Humorous Verse

for

parents

by Amanda Baker

Copyright

Fast Flow Titles

edinburghfft@gmail.com

Notes

For American readers, the word 'fanny' is used in its British context to mean girls' bits. I was hugely confused years ago reading the term 'fanny pack' in a Stephen King novel and realising he meant – what we would call - a 'bum bag'.

fanny – girl front

willy – boy front

bottom – back bit

chips – fries

nappy - diaper

biscuit - cookie

jelly – jell-O

Contents

First, babies have to get out into the world. Advice on how to do this often ignores the fact that pregnancies vary...

1. Whale Music

My friend said she used whale music to help her through the birth

'The group' recommend you pant a lot and channel Mother Earth

Anne planned a pool delivery but got booked for a caesarean

Emily ate the afterbirth though I thought she was vegetarian

Penny did pregnancy Pilates, Yoga, Kung Fu and Tai Chi

She wanted me to go but I said I wasn't free

Lucy's partner rubbed her back so pain would not derail her

But I just screamed my head off and swore like a drunken sailor

And then, despite doing very little, they take over everything...

2. Adoration

We adore our little bundle

Love our darling to bits

Even though all she ever does

Is eats and sleeps and...

... cries

If you already have a child, one of the odd things that happen, on the arrival of a second is that your previously delicate little darling suddenly takes on the proportions of a T-Rex. This happened with my grandson when little sister Matilda arrived. I was an exception that proved a rule weighing in at 10lb when my brother had been a premature 3lb. (See back cover pic.)

3. Matilda Mouse

Matilda was

A tiny wee mouse

Who lived in a house in Bramley

Her daddy was tall her brother was big

Her mum gave enormous cuddles

But

Matilda Mouse

Who lived in that house

Was teeny tiny small

Matilda Mouse

Had a cute little nose

A tiny mouth

Bright little eyes

One floppy ear

And if she cried

You could hardly hear

Because

Matilda mouse

Was a mini mouse

And she lived in a house

In Bramley

Matilda's big brother

Was loud and fun

He liked to jump

He liked to run

He liked to shout

And lark about

And he loved Matilda

The mini mouse

Who shared their house

In Bramley

And Matilda's little bright eyes would follow him

Everywhere he went

Because even though Matilda was

A tiny mouse

Very small

Just a mini mouse

She loved him BIG

In their house

In Bramley

Freud gave us the theory of 'penis envy' though I remain to be convinced how much he really understood about women. However, I was reminded of the idea when my two-year-old grandson, while watching his new sister having her nappy changed, suddenly pulled down his trousers and underpants, adjusted his willy and asked *"where is my fanny?"*

4. Fanny confusion

What's that?

Where's mine?

How does she wee?

That looks silly

Is my fanny

Under my willy?

Penis envy

What's that?

Where's mine?

How does he pee

Up in the air?

I can't do that

It's not fair

While eschewing dishwasher and microwave and many other modern 'essentials' I clearly recall developing an obsessive reliance on my washing machine and worrying about its state of health once I had children.

5. Appeal to an appliance

Oh please don't break pleeease
You are my favourite machine
So good at getting things clean
Don't be mean
Please don't
Make a scene

The boiler is leaking so is the pipe from the sink
So is the loo
They're all in the queue
Ahead of you
All on my list
Of things to do

My daughter lost her shoes
The third pair
It's not fair
Not another repair
Please
I'm tearing out my hair

Dear washing machine I love you
You knew it from the start
Programmed spin cycle upon my heart
I need you now
Though you're not state of the art

Please
START...

The arrival of a friend's small pretty baby prompted my middle daughter – then a teenager – to enquire about her own appearance as a new-born. Well, despite what mothers may see in our hormone induced delusional state – not all babies are photogenic.

6. Not all babies are photogenic

She was a big fat ugly sprog
I cannot tell a lie
The midwives were evasive
Did not look me in the eye
Struck with maternal blindness
I thought she was a cutie
What with all the hormones
My head was tootie fruity

She seemed to be a bonny lass
I held her like a doll
Somehow I failed to notice
She looked just like a troll
Made of large proportions which
Played havoc with my pelvis
She scowled a lot, had blobby cheeks
And thick black hair, like Elvis

It wasn't 'til years later
Looking back at photos blurry
I thought WHAT ON EARTH IS THAT
All bloated cross and furry

She doesn't like this poem
She scowls, she fumes, she curses but
If she slams that door again
I'm going to add three verses

It goes without saying but I will anyway – a smile for a child is free and should always be the default.

7. Smile

Always smile at a child

Take any opportunity

Smiles carry a child for miles

And

Pay dividends on their futures

Frowns don't

This is for all the parents who have tortured themselves with books that hint at the idyllic lives, just over the horizon, that they could have if only they were perfect parents.

8. Perfect Parenting

The parent manual says

She should be sleeping now

I should be having *me* time

Not a blazing partner row

THE BOOK says baby's anxious

But If I'd got it right

He'd be gurgling sweetly

Not howling and uptight

The self-help book says not

To pander to their cries

This other one says that

Is all a pack of lies

This weighty tome advises

A spectacular varied diet

This other one says 'rubbish' as long as

They're full and quiet

I think I'm going to bin

All the books that claim

There's *one* right way to do things

They are driving me insane

I've never been a big fan of chips apart from when I was pregnant with my 3rd child. I put on a huge amount of weight with my 2nd and 3rd pregnancies but I genuinely felt hungry all the time. Once – having eaten a big fish and chip lunch (I've never liked fish and am a vegetarian now) plus ALL the trimmings, I called in for a large cheese pasty on the way back to work. When I sat down at my desk I could have eaten it all again.

9. Chips

Salt 'n vinegar on my lips
Couple of pounds on my hips
I bite, I wait
My heart skips
A beat
As I eat
Golden
Chips

The heart monitor blips
Vital life sign does dips
I sigh I dream
Hot oil drips
I taste
As in haste
I cram

Chips

I will give you some tips
When desire for them grips
Just make a stand
Buy nose clips
Oh sin
Don't give in
To those
Chips

Sometimes your mind just flips
To fantasy fish shop trips
Self-flagellate
Take my advice and get some whips
Or ask a mate
Don't hesitate
It'll be too late
You'll satiate
And then self-hate
With damn
Chipsssssss

And regardless of whether we put on just the perfect amount as I did with my first and lose it all miraculously – our bodies are not the same afterwards. They aren't supposed to be.

10. Before

My fanny's sore my boobs hurt

I don't look like a model

I'm hunched and I have still not lost

That daft ungainly waddle

Mothers in those magazines

Have soft toned flawless skin

And everything is perfect

And everyone is thin

The babies are clean angels

That smile adoringly

At mothers who gaze back

And do not look like me

My partner tried to hug me but

I want to punch his head

Every time he asks

If I'd like tea in bed

I don't want tea I don't want hugs

I want to see the floor

Over my poor stretched tummy

The way I was before...

Despite new priorities and drains on your energy, the same dates roll around and have to be dealt with. When my 3rd child came along I wrote to everyone who'd accumulated on my extensive to-buy-for Christmas list and on whose lists my own children appeared and politely said 'no more'. I'm not doing it anymore and please regard you and yours as off that particular hook too. My note was greeted with cheers and relief and I only annoyed one friend. It was well worth it and has never been regretted.

11. Christmas Crackered

Help help help its Christmas

No I'm not a Turkey

I'm just a normal person

But the world has gone berserk(y)

I want to get my shopping

But the mums have all gone mad

Screaming at their kids

'I'll tell Santa you've been bad'

Everyone looks desperate

We know we have to buy

The perfect partner present but

We don't know where or why

Stores are full of crazy stuff

Predominantly RED

Jingle Bells on auto-play

Is messing with my head

The internet's no better

I ordered stuff in May

Half of it went back

The rest is 'on its way' (apparently!)

Is that Rudolf's nose I see

Glowing in the yard

No the heat is coming off

Some poor sap's credit card

There is no sign of snow

But the weather has gone barmy

We're expecting heatwaves, snow

Hailstones, wind and a tsunami

(More chocolate please I need it

To get me through the season

Normal went to la la land

Along with sense and reason)

Mulled wine mince pies and tinsel

A market with bratwurst

Then suddenly thank goodness

It's January the 1st

There may be some personal hygiene slippage...

12. I Smell

I smell of puke and nappies

And yesterday's mixed goo

I whiff of unwashed hair

And sort of muddling through

My clothes are all a roadmap

Of sticky stains and smears

When I gave birth they must have swapped

My nostrils with my ears

My knickers and my bra

Should be in a museum

My mum would have a heart attack

If she could see 'em

I want to say that hummmm

Isn't really what you think

Bit I have to admit it

I STINK

When my third daughter was still small I got divorced and thereafter dealt more regularly with things that previously I'd delegated when I could. To set a good example I'd pretend that creepy crawlies didn't bother me. The payoff was that I did actually desensitise. However, my youngest daughter went through a stage when her fear of spiders was extreme. This coincided with grandma taking us on holiday to a very spidery cottage where she, fortunately, dealt with the invaders. My mum is from The Caribbean.

13. Granny isn't scared of spiders

My Granny isn't scared of spiders

She comes from a hot country

She says house spiders are our friends

On that we disagree

Granny isn't scared of spiders

She lived near the equator

She says that where she comes from

Spiders are much greater

When I see them scuttling

I want to run and hide

Then in comes granny brush in hand

To usher them outside

Sometimes she scoops them in a pan

Then I know their fate

Shell open up the window

And defenestrate

My gran comes from a hot place

Where spiders are immense

If I lived there I would build

A massive spider fence

We like to swim we like to climb

We're skaters and bike riders

But

The thing I love about my gran

She is not scared of spiders

I wish I was like granny with

Such bravery inside her

That way I would not mind a bit

Meeting with a spider

Granny says I am funny

And If I could only see

Spiders are so tiny that

They are afraid of me

The simplest desires can be thwarted.

14. A cup of tea
(becomes an insurmountable challenge)

I want a cup of tea

Easy

I thought

Now I'm on the loo

With my baby

On my knee

Attached to me

Feeding

My toddler is swinging

From the door handle

Weeeeeee

Laughing at me

No tea...

And things you used to take for granted or think of as part of you can drift away...

15. I used to read Maya Angelou

I used to read Maya Angelou

Now I'm mesmerised by

The subtle nuances and

Denouement of

The Elves and the Shoemaker

The Cat in the Hat

I used to watch film noir

Now I consume

Endless episodes

Concerning

Psychotic trains and

Headache-coloured puppets

I used to eat Italian

Now I vacuum up

Leftovers with

My scabby mouth

Spaghetti shapes or

Limp eggy bread

I used to have a social life

Now I sit in homes

That look like mine

Child swamps clogged with

Toys - food - clothes and

Talk of sleepless nights

I used to dress to advantage

Now I don't know

It's hard to tell

Because I can't remember

The last time I

Looked in a mirror…

Simple bodily functions can rule your life to the point of mania. Yes, I've interchanged 'diaper' and 'nappy' here but who'd forego the chance of nice alliteration.

16. Diaper download desperation

He's squirming and squinting

I think he will pooh

It's long overdue

When will he pooh

He is gurning and twisting

He's smothered in lotion

Will he chill soon and

Bring forth a motion

I'm exhausted I am angst

I am frothing with frustration

I have that new syndrome

Diaper download desperation

You cannot comprehend

How elated I'd be

If he would give in and

Drop it in that nappy

It's consuming my life

Nothing else matters

Unless he poops soon

My life is in tatters

It's been three full days

I'm going off my head

I'm obsessed with his bottom

I'm coming to dread

Clean nappies

He's done it, It's happened

I'll ring all my friends

Who'd ever have thought

That Purgatory ends

I want to celebrate

Proclaim the great news

Nothing else counts

As long as he poohs

When I was doing informal childminding to pay the bills that writing rarely covers, I met a child who was gifted, possibly a genius. The beauty was, his parents hadn't noticed. In most cases, it is parental delusion. A sibling or starting school usually cures the parents and takes the pressure off the child.

17. The Genius

Max is a genius,

Friends look at us and sigh

They're often busy when we call

And I've worked out why

I do not want to gloat

But it's obvious to me

He'll need to go to uni

By the time he's three

We worry about sending him

To ordinary school

Where he'd have to mix with every

Snot-nosed basic fool

I ensure he is inspired

Each moment of the day

Hang on his every utterance

Encourage structured play

Even his defecations

Don't smell like other boys'

His food is all organic

And so are all his toys

We don't allow loud noises

That would be remiss of us

Yes, I'm slightly bonkers

But it's worth it for a genius

Of course, we all hope we are not the parent of the 'other' sort of stand-out child.

18. The monster is mine

PLEASE be good

Don't hit or punch or bite

Please be an angel

Don't put my friends to flight

Please can you be cute this once

Not snotty loud and rude

Be the poppet not the one

They all want to exclude

I love you so much and

You try I know that's plain

But just this once please let it be

Another kid who's the

PAIN

Once your child starts to read, try easy fun verse. I've rarely gone into a school without being armed with T.S.Eliot's *Macavity the Mystery Cat* or Benjamin Zephaniah's brilliant Football Mad poem *Clever Trevor*. To that I add some of my own.

This piece was written during a school literacy project. The children wrote descriptive pieces about that day's lunch menu and I promised I'd 'eat' the best pieces. I'm not a fan of jelly but the funkiest descriptive piece was about that school pudding which was served in rectangular portions. I ate it as promised and then wrote this poem to prove to the children you can write about anything.

19. Rectangular Jelly!

You get rectangular jelly in my new school

They make it in the school canteen

You get rectangular jelly in my new school

Ruby red or emerald green

Perhaps potatoes will be star shaped

And apples will be square

You'll get a surprise if you try to sit down

Because a table will be a chair

Will the gravy be made of chocolate

In this crazy miss-shaped place

Are the children made of marmalade

Do the teachers come from outer space

Were the walls built boldly of beetroot

Do the cooks make curry flavoured honey

Are the radishes blue in triangle stew

If you ask me it's all a bit funny

Maybe water will be custard

And bananas will be flat

You get rectangular jelly in my new school

What do you think of that

As a parent, there are some things we get sick of hearing ourselves say.

20. Don't

Don't scream don't shout don't stamp don't pout

Don't scratch don't hit just sit a bit

Don't grind or glare or point and stare

Don't strop or sulk or turn into the Hulk

Don't play with snot or pick you bot

Don't whack him in the face or be a disgrace

Don't sleep too much don't wake don't cry

Don't eat boogers don't keep asking why

Don't start

Don't give up

Don't speak to strangers

Don't ignore Aunt Anne

Don't get stressed

Don't forget your homework

Don't speak to me like that

Don't lie to me

Don't stay out late

Don't be anti-social

Don't go out half-dressed

Don't come in drunk

Don't miss an opportunity

Don't take too many risks

Don't be immature

Don't grow up too quickly…

When our darlings go to school it's not possible that we are going to like all of their friends.

21. Be my fwend

If you want to be my fwend

You must go and see

If your mum will ask my mum

If I can come for tea

If Sophie Nixon kicks me

You smack her really hard

And if the teachers catch you say

I wasn't in the yard

I know that you've got cake

You are supposed to share

If you don't give me some

I'm going to pull your hair

Be my bestest ever pal

We'll be fwends for ever

Unless Jane's got her Susie doll or

I get sweets off Heather

Whether you have one child or five, there is no getting away from this state of affairs.

22. TIRED

There is a level of TIRED you do not comprehend

You've never really been at the absolute end

Of that tether

You think you're prepared when a child fills the crib

And all your emotions crazily ad lib

But you're not

There is tired upon tired there's drained shattered zombified

There is upside down inside out blank and stupefied

You'll see

There is wiped-out worn weary bleary droopy and fatigued

Obliterated messed up and dead beat

For starters

Nothing quite compares to the tiredness which attends

The pitter-patter

Of those

Tiny

Feet

Friendships at school are, for the most part, wonderful.
Children all have their little foibles which are endlessly
fascinating. Some I remember well.

23. Rosie prefers mayonnaise

Rosie doesn't put sauce on chips
She prefers Mayonnaise
The triplets don't like chips at all
So their daddy says

Eve likes savoury rice but
She's not that keen on bread
Amy says that when you sleep spiders crawl in your mouth
And wander round your head
(Which is why you're not hungry in the morning!)

Lauren always eats her crusts
Even so, her hair is straight
They all seem to enjoy spag bol
Which mutinies off the plate

Time devours the years
They'll be grown in just two blips
But I'll always remember Rosie
Liked mayonnaise on her chips!

When your fragile, little precious turns into a toddler and learns the word 'NO!' and how to have a tantrum it is worth contemplating that this is a prelude to the teenage years except then they will be much bigger and they won't have afternoon naps. You may struggle to get them out of bed at all...

24. You don't understand

I just knew you'd say that
I see that you don't care
You think I'm being childish
And that is just not fare
You don't understand about... my hair

Everyone else's hair does this
And mine always does that
All the 'in' girls in my class are thin
And I am fat
But I wouldn't expect *you* to care about all that

You give him more attention than me
I know that he's your pet
You've ruined my life, you don't care
And now I am upset.
I really don't know how much *worse* my life could get

No one else at my school does this
Wash up, clean my room - give me a break
You're always getting at me
How much more can I take
Just leave me alooone for heaven's sake

(phone) "Oh hi Jane... Yeah I know
Oh that's fab, that's really *great*
Are Beth and Nick going?
Uhu – yeah I know – I can't wait
Did you see her? Yeah whatever
Ok see you in school
Yeah – I got it – gotta go now – ok that's cool"

Nobody loves me, I've got no friends
But I never get to have my way
I'll be leaving home soon
You don't listen to what I say
And you'll be sooooo sorry when I've gone away (?!*)

The other girls have boyfriends
And I am by myself
If this goes on much longer
I'll be left on the shelf
You don't understand cos you were never like this yourself

If you cared you would listen
And help and be kind
It's very hard being me
I've got lots on my mind.
If I can't do what they do – I'll get left behind

(door bell) Gotta go! I'll have tea later
Susan's here I gotta fly
Could you wash my favourite jeans
And make sure that they're dry
I need them for the morning - see you mum - Bye!

Sometimes it can feel overwhelming. Trying to carve out a moment when you do something you'd like, seems a distant unobtainable luxury.

25. Drowning in my Family

She stands in the doorway hunched, just pre-nuclear. Her hair is not right.

The Princess's faultlessly coloured mouth pouts, threatening to quiver. Upper facial expressions are not always easy to fathom as the eyebrows have been plucked into immaculate arches. Is she permanently slightly surprised? I have no idea; she has become a teenage enigma to me. I was not allowed to be a teenager. I am in awe of her willpower.

Slender hip against the wall, arms folded, designer trainers, which should be off in the house, scuff the floor, like a bull preparing to charge. My fingers hover over the keyboard. If I continue there will be a row and even though she might stomp off leaving me free for maybe fifteen minutes, my fingers will wilt and become detached from my brain. Whatever was there will have vaporised. On the other hand, if I give in, offering further pampering and attention, will the ultimate outcome not be the same? Shouldn't the consideration be the effect on her character of these two different courses of action rather than calculating the number of minutes lost to my addiction - writing?

The princess senses I am losing my train of thought.

"Muuuuum!" she grumbles.

"MUM!" she snaps. Not as aggressively as she would have done if she thought the battle was lost.

Princess glowers at me, scanning me critically. Looking directly at her, I smile. Maybe she's right, appearance is important. I press 'save'. Stand up. Keep the smile. I will spend more time on her hair. She relaxes her shoulders.

Having created a cardboard bed for her stuffed horse, tissue clothes for her extensive collection of beanie babies and transformed her bedroom into toy heaven, my middle daughter crashes down two flights of stairs. She takes four at a time, the last six in a heroic leap. Two broken arms, one fall through a plate glass door, a bloody encounter with a pebbledash wall, mean nothing to her. Even a disaster involving a metal climbing frame, Wellington boots and another trip to A&E has not deterred her from hurling her limbs towards hard surfaces with great energy. She lands in a heap - grinning. Physically she is brave. Outside school it is painfully easy to tell from a distance if her day was bad. Playground taunts or difficulties with more worldly 'friends' are projected through raised shoulders, a drag in her walk, her chin almost on her chest. On better days she bounces towards me and I am able to breathe.

She is the current playground pariah. It is her turn. Again. On these occasions I look into her face and I see in the deep pools of her hazel/green eyes that it is, despite my assurances to the contrary, the end of the world. She wants a duck for her birthday!

I've just sat down to try to work again. Why is it impossible to have a duck for her birthday? She needs to know *now*. I decide that if we discuss this problem whilst cooking it will save time. What will I do with the saved time? Perhaps if I add it to all the other saved time I could have a week off.

During the 'environmental requirements of ducks' exchange, I cook pasta. I calculate whether to do enough for the adults to eat later if my husband arrives home. Will it be inedible by then? Is it sufficient anyway as an offering for a man who has been at meetings? Perhaps it's ok as long as there is a salad. He's not keen on salad but it looks good. There is no salad. Cooked pasta does not keep well. Really I know this.

Princess saunters into the kitchen, grimaces at her sister, asks without hope, what's for tea, throws a look of disdain at me, tosses her beautiful hair - exits. The pasta boils. Duck Girl is cross. The duck issue is not being taken seriously enough. I am worrying about adult food, resenting further kitchen confinement, feeling guilty about the resentment. Has the last paragraph worked or will it need to be rewritten? Do I need a bath? When did I last wash my hair? Will Treasure eat her tea or have I allowed too many biscuits? Is there anything in the freezer? Can I get away without shopping for another two days? A house with this many people always needs bloody cleaning. The phone rings, I am about to yell, "Leave it" but am too slow.

Treasure has the mouthpiece upside down, giggling into the plastic.
"Ask them to call back," I yell.
Duck Girl dangles the phone in triumph.
"It's grandma – she says it will only take a minute"
She smirks.
Brightly I say we're in the middle of tea, equally brightly grandma says she will be quick and tells everything fast, garbled so that meaning is lost and things have to be repeated. I smell gas. Boiled-over water extinguished the flame. Treasure is dancing in the kitchen. Too near the cooker (?) with her wooden-brick trolley. She wants another biscuit, unimpressed by the promise of pasta.

Princess snarls at Duck Girl over the mediocre food. Treasure vies for their attentions. She is the extra one. The one there was no need for, no logical explanation, no rationale. My boss had not thought she was a good idea and suddenly decided that my job – I – was 'redundant'. Law firms know how to get away with these things.

Treasure is beloved of all. Although amazingly self-reliant she will not tolerate being ignored. You would never know by looking at the chocolate button eyes, the dimples, the sumptuous chestnut curls that she is a sleep tormentor. Until recently she'd often wake during the night up to six times. I know all the rules about sleep-training toddlers, leaving them to cry for specified times, about going in but not giving too much attention - but with this child it was - harder.

For eight and a half years there was no new baby in the house and suddenly the cot was tenanted again. Such smiles, such gurgles, such cuddles. On the rare occasions that she really cries the family collectively tenses, we blame each other if Treasure is unhappy. Someone made too much noise, someone did the wrong thing, someone failed to cut out the scratchy labels from the pure cotton vests, someone allowed the nurse to be too rough with the needle. Between the four of us we just about lavish enough love. To leave her to cry at night, the darkest time, the time of least strength and resolve – was not possible for me. It is amazing how long one can go without proper sleep. This morning we watched *The Little Mermaid* video at 5 am – a lie-in. When allowed my choice we watch *Old Bear*.

I try sneaking to the PC. She has radar. I am located. She scrambles onto my knee, smiling, chattering. If I attempt anything as foolish as finishing the sentence, two soft warm hands are sweetly, firmly pressed onto either side of my face, my cheeks are clamped in the lovely vice of her little paws. The gentle, determined pressure increases as she turns my head towards its proper object. I smell her sweaty hair and sticky skin. We make eye contact; she rewards me with a bigger smile – a smile to die for. Her clothes are filthy.

I never bothered with a dishwasher, microwave or other unfriendly contraptions but have an obsessive attachment to my washing machine. It works unceasingly for me. It does not complain. It is my partner. It has not ever let me down in the years since I bought it during a lunch break, with a work bonus, despite almost daily abuse. Memories of mother's titanic twin tub, granny's reminiscences of mangles, send shivers down my spine. An Irish acquaintance told of washing clothes for a family of seven in a stream. I love my washing machine.

I love my cardigan. The current cardigan was bought in a local charity shop. Treasure and I are clothed from these Aladdin's caves. My cardigan is cream. It is large. It is a cable knit. It is warm. It loves me. It is the clothing equivalent of chocolate and hugs. I wear it in the afternoons when the house is quiet if Treasure has her nap and I cannot justify central heating for one.

Treasure wakes from her nap and needs food. Then there is the feeding frenzy that occurs when the girls battle through the door after school. They are *starving* even though they know of the children in Africa. Then proper tea. The fourth is the adult meal. He is not fussy but sometimes he has 'no appetite' or 'had a late lunch' or will 'eat later' or 'will eat' and the meal is put on the table and he has to 'just finish something' until the meal expires there. I try to resist calculating the wasted time in the kitchen. Many a meal has had side-salads scrapped off the plate so that the dinner can be kept in the oven. When it is finally consumed it may as well have come out of a pet food can. It is viscid, grey, congealed round the edges. He knows he shouldn't complain or ask for an alternative so grudgingly he picks. Exploiting the opportunity of a potty emergency, he decants it into the bin. He does not openly hold the culinary disappointment against me. I may hold it against him.

At bedtime he is ready to play with Treasure. I do not want play now I want calm but that is unfair because he has not had his *turn*, his smiles, his rewards for being funny, entertaining, jovial. He will bath Treasure – for me.

It is all finally done; taxiing to ballet, homework, clearing up, establishing positions over Princess's social commitments, perhaps I will slip down to the pc now. Could I just fetch PJs? Where are the bath toys? Is he washing her hair? Does she need her medicine? Could I just fetch a clean towel because he is busy with her? I brush aside an entreaty from Duck Girl; ignore pointed remarks from Princess about my parental failure to understand the ultra-importance of regular sleepovers, and jog for the towel to save time. There is still hope. While he is undressing Treasure, could I just check the temperature of the bath water? I do, which is quicker than asking why he couldn't do it. He has a work problem could

I go through it with him later – yes of course - and with a smile! While I am there could I pass the shampoo and by the way could I stay because Treasure does not like having her hair washed? He must not be responsible for unpopular activities.

The moment comes. It doesn't always. Princess is blasting electronic messages to other princesses explaining how she is imprisoned in this awful place with ridiculous people who are mean to her / do not understand or care about her. One day all the princesses will escape together. Duck Girl is in her room, sulking or creating. Husband and Treasure are in the sitting room with music on; she is dancing to applause and squealing when she is thrown in the air. If I go in I will complain about inappropriate pre-bedtime activities so I don't go in.

The bathroom door is ajar and curling steam tempts me in. Treasure's bath. It is my chance. I sniff my armpits, not just my chance – my destiny. I jam the hot tap on full to top-up the bath, remove plastic fish, legless doll, sponge crab, something indescribable. Carefully I close the door.

Pee urgently, strip quickly. Dare I lock the door? Finding a door locked with me on the other side is liable to send any member of the family into a fit of indignation. I lock it. Duck Girl thumps overhead. I slip in.

Princess clicks the keyboard furiously. Treasure dances and squeals, fractious and off-key now but still unaware of my betrayal. I slide down. The hot water, like my cardigan, adores me. "Where have you been?" it murmurs. I am enveloped up to my neck. My muscles sing out the hallelujah chorus. No one knows I am here. Has anyone ever known luxury like this?

For no reason I stare at the ceiling.
No thumping.
Ominous.
Then I am startled by a sharp rapping on the door. The handle is rattled.
"Why can't I have a duck?"
Briefly I wonder if you could keep a duck in the back yard of Victorian terrace...

I let my head slip under the water.

Bringing children into a world that seems so precarious can feel daunting. Last Shrove Tuesday I posted this poem, in the form of a secular prayer, on my blog.

26. Make pancakes not war

Make pancakes not war

Make love don't fight

Talk it over

Have a cuppa

Be still

Be the light

Don't shoot to kill

Plant sunflowers,

Grow crops, fix the world

You can't call back

Harsh words

Once they've been hurled

Hold hands in soft silence

Pick fruit

Row a boat

Slow down

Observe

Watch bath toys afloat

Make peace with joyful noise

Have a hug

Be my friend

Don't go on

Like this

Stumbling to the end

Let the sum of your

Happiness

Outweigh

Your despair

Make pancakes

AND love if you dare...

Also by Amanda Baker

<u>Adult novels</u>

The Companion Contract

Eating the Vinyl

<u>Dystopian novella</u>

Zero One Zero Two

<u>Epic environmental poetry story</u>

Casey & the Surfmen

(also available as an audio story on bandcamp)

<u>Adventure trilogy (8 – 12yrs)</u>

bk1. *Eleanor & Dread Mortensa*

bk2. *Eleanor the Dragon Witch & the Time Twisting Mirror*

bk3. *Eleanor & the Dragon Runt*

<u>Picture book in verse for little readers</u>

Ella & the Knot Fairies

Sort of autobiography

Maybe I'm not a Pigeon

Anthologies that include Amanda's work

The Iron book of New Humorous Verse (poetry)

ROOT anthology (short stories)

Printed in Poland
by Amazon Fulfillment
Poland Sp. z o.o., Wrocław

50484513R00042